BIKER'S LOST BABY

BWWM Mafia Romance

Jolie Damman

CONTENTS

CHAPTER 1

I didn't even know what I was doing at this party. It was for rich people only. That was why I was feeling so out of place. But my friend was here and she was supposed to help me with feeling better about this, and I couldn't see her anywhere.

To be honest, I didn't exactly enter the place where the party was happening yet. I was just outside the building, looking at it from side to side, and up and down, and imagining how it was possible that people built that place and made it look like what it was.

It was modern, fancy, luxurious, and pretty much every other adjective I could think of. The kind of place that made me think less about myself the moment I first stepped inside it, which I didn't know when it was going to happen. I could see some partygoers already leaving their cars to go to the party, and they were all laughing and chatting and having a blast.

As for me, I didn't even know if I was going to make it all the way to the party so that I could be with my friend. Since the place was mostly made of windows and glass doors, I was hoping I was going to see her from the outside, but there were also so many people... I just couldn't see her among them.

In the meantime, I was trying to control my breathing, and trying not to have too many crushes here in this place. The men that were coming to the party were so confident, so handsome, and so everything I liked that I just couldn't stop stealing glances at them, even though I knew I shouldn't be.

If there was something I promised myself when I was younger and I thought I could finally have a grasp on was what having a relationship was like, and I said I would never fall in love again with anyone.

I had just finished breaking up with my previous boyfriend and it was a nightmare. He thought he could control me, that he could do anything to me, and he was making my life a living hell. I was just so happy that he wasn't a part of it anymore, but that didn't change anything. I just kept thinking about him, thinking about how much he affected my life and also thinking about what I was going to do now without someone to help me.

The truth was that even though I had a stable job, it didn't pay me enough. Certainly not enough to pay the bills and the food and everything else I needed to survive.

Just thinking about that, I decided to shake my head and not think about those things anymore. One of the things I said I was going to do at this party was that I was going there, going to see my friend, and I was going to have a blast with her. After all, that was one of the things she promised we were going to do.

She had a better job than me. She was a fashion advisor and one of the best at it. Did I feel envious of it? Not at all, but it was something that made me think about my life and everything else that was associated with it. One of the things that I knew would never change, something I thought would never happen, but which did, was the fact that I had a son.

He was the most beautiful, sweet thing in the world, but I couldn't deny that he was also one of my sources of stress. Even though I knew he could be better, he wasn't – at least, not to me.

I didn't like thinking about him that way, so I shooed that thought out of my mind right at this moment.

He didn't make my life a living hell and it was better with him around, but there was no denying that he was spoiled. I thought I wasn't helping with putting him in that direction, but it happened, and I couldn't do anything about it. I couldn't change it anymore.

No matter what I did, he was always going to look at me and wonder what happened to his father. He was going to keep asking me why I broke up with him, even though it was the only thing I could do at that moment so that I didn't explode.

Now, we were living in a very rundown and dingy apartment, and it was the kind of place I just didn't want to go back to. I left him with my mother, who was at least living with me and was helping me with taking care of the apartment.

But even then, that meant I also had to keep working so that I could keep putting food on the table and she didn't have to feel hungry. I loved her. She was my mother and I would do anything for her, and I was glad that she was helping me recently by taking care of my son when I was working and, some other times, going to places like this, but there was no denying that she also put some extra weight in my life.

I took a deep breath and decided to enter the building. A guard stood outside of it and he looked at me as though he knew I wasn't supposed to be here. But even if that was what he was thinking, I was going to prove him wrong.

After all, I did my best before coming here. I groomed myself, bought a different dress just for this party, did my hair, put on better makeup than what I had before, and also even bought better perfume so that the first thing that everyone thought about me was how good it smelled.

The guard was a tall man, with a cap, and he wore a mask, most likely because he was afraid of the pandemic. But just like everyone else, we had been jabbed several times, took all the doses, and we should all be protected against the virus.

That wasn't going to stop him, though, from wearing a mask at the party. He was one of the few that wore one. Everyone else going into the building didn't have masks on, and at least that was one of the few reasons why I didn't feel completely out of place yet. I mean, I kind of did, but at least that was something I could relate to them.

He was also black, just like I was, though his skin tone was slightly darker than mine. I didn't think much about that, just that everyone else in the party, other than the guard, was white.

I supposed that was one of the few things that should have helped me to spot my friend among the partygoers. Considering that everyone here was white or mixed race, then another black woman among them should have helped me with finding her, right?

But it was also likely she was nowhere near the party. More often than not, she was late to do anything.

In the meantime, I just couldn't stop thinking about my son and if he was doing okay. I knew that he had some kind of condition that made him think differently. Sometimes, he behaved so weirdly. Sometimes, he acted as though he didn't even know who I was.

Sometimes, he also acted as though he couldn't see anything, even though I took him to the eye doctor so many times to check his eyes and she always told me that everything was okay with them.

"Your name, Ms.?" The guard asked, and I gave him my name, which he checked on the list he was holding in his hands. It was a white, single paper sheet with a list of names, and I knew that my name had to be on it. The problem was that I still couldn't stop feeling nervous, my fingers moving and twitching slightly. It was one of the things about me that always showed how nervous I was.

His eyes checked the list of names and then he looked at me and I gave him my ID. The first thing I thought was going to happen was that he wasn't going to find my name on the list, he was going to ask me to turn around and leave, and then I would ask my friend so many questions, pretty much cornering her, that I knew I would lose my friendship with her.

But then, he looked up, giving me my ID back. I put it back in my shoulder bag and then I smiled when he said, "You can go in, Ms. Crawford."

CHAPTER 2

Harry

I didn't know what I was doing in this place. There was a friend of mine who asked me to come here, but it wasn't for me. I had a lot of money, I was supposed to be feeling at home with these people, but I didn't. I just felt so different. I felt out of place.

The only time when I didn't feel out of place was when I was sitting on my motorcycle. It was a sturdy, heavy motorcycle and it was the best thing in the world to me. Whenever I sat on it, I felt as though time stopped and I could think about everything clearly. When I was with my fingers gripping the handlebars, I felt I was in control of my life.

That was one of the reasons why I couldn't stop thinking about going outside for a smoke. I knew what people would think of me if I did that, though. I was supposed to be the CEO of a major company in the state, but I didn't feel like running anything – not anything that involved managing so many people and making them think that I was going to make the company soar to higher levels.

I was a biker, or at least, I was trying to be one. The men that looked up to me were all supporting me, and I felt that they were the least fake people I had ever met in my life. And being 32 years old, I had met a lot of fake people, including my wife.

My wife... I couldn't think about her without feeling like she was looking at me all the time. Even now, when nothing of importance was happening at the party, people mingling and just arriving, she was always all over me. Always coming for me. Always trying to control everything I did, and even pretending that the spark between us was still there.

But that was the thing. It wasn't there anymore and I didn't think it would ever change. Just one other reason to think that there wasn't such a thing as love. Just thinking about it... I didn't even want to be thinking about it, to be honest.

It was nothing more than a waste of time, especially when someone else was at the party.

She didn't have to believe me about it, and I didn't think she ever would, but she was the most stunning woman in the world. The problem was that she already had a son, and he was weird and a handful to her at the same time. Sometimes he acted as though he was an autist, other times he was a little devil, and other times I couldn't even begin to grasp what was going on in his mind.

I wanted to take him to a psychiatrist, but I couldn't. That would mean initiating a conversation with Antez, that black goddess that stole my dreams and made it so I couldn't stop thinking about her, even when my wife was nearby, like she was right now, oscillating around me, smelling me, trying to talk to me and make people think that we were still in love.

It just wasn't going to happen, and nothing of that would ever change.

Not to mention that she said so many times she wasn't looking for someone like me. I ran a motorcycle club and I was the president of it. I was rough. I knew what hardship was like, even though I was also a billionaire and had been to so many places she would never even dream of.

The thing about me was that I didn't look pleasant. My looks were rough, I had tattoos on my body, scars, my skin was slightly textured, and, overall I always looked grumpy and as though I was going to kill someone.

It was no wonder that I was pretty much alone with my wife, who kept on grabbing my hand, trying to take me here and there, to talk to this person and that other guy, but every time she did that, she only managed to annoy me more.

Also, Antez would never even look at me. She was finally with the friend that invited me to come here. My wife was one of the masterminds behind this, but Aksa was the one that, in the end, convinced me to come to this party so that I could feel out of place and as though everyone was judging me.

That was why I was holding my wine glass in my hand and trying not to break it at the same time. It was so delicate and so small, and if I didn't handle it properly, the wine in it would spill out.

In the meantime, I was looking at Antez and I knew she would never look at me. Time was passing, nothing was happening, someone was talking to me and I was talking back, but that was about it.

I just couldn't stop looking at Antez without feeling my cock twitching slightly in my pants. I knew what my wife would think, but looking at her, I didn't see her as my wife anymore.

I took a deep breath in, glancing to the other side when I realized that Antez just looked in my direction. Was it brief? Did she actually look at me or was I only imagining things? I didn't know, but that got me thinking, it made me think, and when I looked back to see if I was right about that, she was actually looking elsewhere, this time still talking to her friend.

This was all so overwhelming and annoying. For a moment, I really thought that Antez was looking at me, but that couldn't be the case. I knew what happened to her. She had one of the most traumatic breakups with her boyfriend, who was also the father of her child.

The asshole was so who he was that he didn't even want to pay her to keep taking care of the boy. He ran away to another state and the police were still going after him. But just before he did that, though, I gave him a message. I didn't know if it reached him, but I hoped it did. If it did, he knew that my men were looking for him. Eventually, we would sniff him out and take care of the huge problem he created.

For Antez's sake, I wouldn't kill him when that happened, but

I would teach him a lesson he would never forget. Just thinking about him, about all the afflictions he caused on his former girlfriend, I fisted my hands. If there was something that I wanted to do right now other than to kiss Antez, it was to be with my fingers choking that man.

I continued looking at Antez, hoping that she was going to look back and show me I wasn't hallucinating when I saw that, but nothing happened. In the meantime, my wife was already poking her hand on my chest, drawing my attention to her. It was the only way she could manage to make me do that, and it annoyed me as much as pretty much everything else about this party.

Sometimes, she was so oblivious to what I was feeling. I considered so many times just saying to her face how much I despised her, but I wasn't going to do that. The truth was that I wasn't a monster even though I had killed so many times in my life. I was someone used to killing people, to torturing them, to drugs, and pretty much everything else. I knew how dangerous I was, and I was also aware that my position as CEO of the company was one of the few things preventing the police from locking me up.

And then, I noticed her looking at me again, and was I hallucinating or something like that? I didn't think that was the case, but I couldn't know for sure. What I knew for sure was that some heat was rising to her cheeks and they were blushing. It was almost imperceptible, considering the distance between us and her skin color – something that I didn't like to think about that way.

The fact that she was black didn't have anything to do with my love. She was who she was and it just didn't have anything to do with anything.

Regardless, that was something I would never say to her.

She was also so curvy that I just wanted to be moving my hands on her curves, to feel every part of her, but I couldn't do that. Not when my wife was still all over me, still trying to talk to me as I tried to reply to her without making it look like I was only coming up with words that didn't mean anything.

Our stare lasted only a couple seconds, but it felt like it lasted much more than that.

I didn't know what that meant, but I was a man of action, and after seeing that and deciding that this party was so boring that I just had to do something to make it less so, I was already planning on how I was going to develop this situation and act on it.

My curiosity was killing me right now.

CHAPTER 3

Antez

I didn't know what I was thinking, that guy staring at me as though he just noticed something funny about me. I wasn't going to deny that I had some self-esteem problems. The moment I noticed his cold gaze on me, the first thing I thought was that something was wrong with my appearance. Maybe it was the purple dress, my hair, my makeup, or something along those lines.

Maybe I was just imagining things that weren't happening, too.

In the meantime, it wasn't like I was fully alone. I couldn't be, considering the number of people around me, everyone chatting and having the time of their lives. Aksa was also with me, chatting about her fashion choices, how much her clients loved her work, and pretty much everything about her.

About her only.

It wasn't that she was too self-centered or anything like that, but when she was in the mood to talk about her life, it was impossible to put a damper on it. I wasn't going to say anything about it, just letting her keep running her mouth as though this party was all about her.

In truth, it wasn't. This party was for the company, and the man that just looked at me? He was none other than the CEO. At least, he pretended that he was and sometimes he also pretended he wasn't. I didn't know much about him, other than the few times we exchanged a couple of words without really talking, but he liked his motorcycle and the motorcycle club that he ran.

Someone else ran the company for him. I often asked myself how they managed to do that only to always realize that it was pretty simple. He didn't run the company because he didn't have to. As CEO, he didn't have to do much.

His life was so conflicting. I'd always thought that bikers were poor and rugged, but he was different. He was a billionaire and a biker at the same time. I didn't know how his business partners looked at it and thought that investing in his company was a good idea.

Nothing of this made any sense.

Other than the fact that he had indeed been looking at me. I didn't know what he was thinking, but he was indeed looking at me, and I couldn't help but feel some heat rising to my cheeks.

And I supposed it was at that moment that Aksa noticed something was different about me. It wasn't that something was wrong with me, but that she just noticed something was off.

She stopped saying what she was saying, putting her hands on her waist as she said, "Antez, are you even listening to what I'm saying?"

I cleared my throat, realizing that I should have been paying more attention to what she was saying. After all, she was my friend, she helped me a lot, and even though sometimes she looked so self-centered, more often than not she really cared about me, too.

"Sorry."

She took a deep breath, looking where I was looking before. "If it's something about Harry, then you are obligated to tell me about it. I just want you to know that I'm here for you, even though I sometimes look like I'm not."

I took a deep breath in, already feeling bad about what I was thinking before. Even though she was only talking about herself all the time, she noticed that I was thinking about the same thing over and over, obsessing over it.

I didn't even know what to say about this. I knew that I had a crush on Harry, but bringing it up and talking about it with my friend didn't seem like a good idea.

I took a sip of my wine and then I finally replied, "Yeah, it's about him."

"What about him?" She asked, and then she added, "If you feel that anything is going to happen between you two, I'm sorry to disappoint you. He really isn't the right kind of man for you. You still remember what happened between you and your ex, right? He is worse."

It was like a punch to my gut, and I felt as though I was going to pass out. I never thought that Aksa would just compare Harry to my ex. I knew he was bad, but I didn't think he was so bad that she thought they were on the same level.

"It's nothing about that. I just find him a little hot, that's all," I said as she shook her head, putting her hand on my shoulder and then leading me out of there. I had no idea where we were going, but she was adamant about it, pushing me forward with confidence. I had to be mindful not to drop the wine glass I was holding. It was good, but there were so many things going on in my mind right now I just couldn't enjoy the drink.

Some seconds later, we were outside when something appeared to have caught her attention. Or rather, it was someone coming to talk to her that did that. She clasped her hands together and smiled, saying with joy, "Oh, yeah, I definitely know what you're talking about."

I didn't.

And without saying anything about it, she just went off with whoever had come to talk to her. She didn't even look in my direction, but she waved her hand to tell me she wanted me to wait.

The good thing about it was that being outside meant I didn't have to deal with anyone. Didn't have to talk to anyone, and it was quiet and so much so I could even hear the chirp of the crickets in the bushes.

I was just turning around when I heard a loud motorcycle

riding fast in my direction, splashing water over me, and wetting and destroying my dress. The first thing I did was to drop my wine glass, which broke into a million pieces on the hard floor in front of the building where the party was taking place.

I snapped my head to the motorcycle, noticing that the guy that was riding on it was from one of the motorcycle clubs in the city. His patch was quite distinct, too. It had a snake, a dragon, and wings. He wasn't from Harry's gang but from another.

Now that I was remembering them, I also remembered something else. I had heard Harry saying something along the lines of that gang helping my ex to escape. They didn't know that for certain, though, so they weren't able to act on it. They were also not going to start a war with another motorcycle club over something that didn't have to do with them.

It wasn't like their more common quarrels, where they fought over territory and that sort of thing.

But that didn't matter right now. I already came to this party looking so out of place, and now I looked ridiculous.

My dress was all wet, I dropped the wine glass, and it was difficult for me to even keep my balance. If I didn't do something about that, I would fall over on my ass, and pretty much everyone at the party, who was already looking outside after I let out a scream, would be laughing at me.

My dress was so wet that I knew I was going to have to go back to my apartment and tell Aksa about what happened.

I hated that biker even though I didn't know anything about him. He should have been more aware of what was in front of him before riding past me so fast on his motorcycle.

And even after he noticed what he did, he didn't turn around and come back to me to say he was sorry. Rather, he just continued to ride and then entered the boulevard, heading somewhere. I didn't know where he was going, but I did get his motorcycle's plate number and I was going to keep that information in mind.

It wasn't that I was planning on having my revenge against him, but that at least it was something I could remember so that, in case that information was useful, I could use it.

The splash of the water on me was so strong it almost knocked me down, and I felt a pair of hands supporting me up so that I didn't fall on my ass. It was the same guy from before, the one that was looking at me.

Harry. Harry 'Punisher' Adams. 'Punisher' was his nickname and he liked that people called him that. I thought it was ridiculous and another reason why I knew we would never fall in love.

We just didn't have any chemistry, even though he was being chivalrous right now, holding me up so that I didn't make a fool of myself. But it was too late. I had to run away from the party as soon as possible so that fewer people noticed what happened.

Some were even taking out their phones and snapping photos of me, something that angered me so much I just wanted to go up there and start to slap their faces until they said how sorry they were.

CHAPTER 4

Harry

Didn't think she was going to be almost falling on her ass. I was holding her up carefully, trying everything I could so that she didn't think I was going to hurt her, too. I didn't think that was going to happen, but with women as delicate as she was, I couldn't be sure.

When she was standing on her two feet again, I noticed her eyes looking over my shoulders as though she was scanning the guests at the party. She was probably wondering if they were looking at her and finding this funny, but they weren't.

For the first few moments, some people were indeed looking. Maybe there was a chuckle here or there, but not much more than that. Now? Now they were all cackling, chatting, and behaving like they didn't see anything.

After all, could they even see her as more than the person she was? I was probably partial about this, but Antez was nothing short of stunning. I would see her wherever she was and whatever she was doing. It wasn't love at first sight, but there was no denying that she was my type.

Just thinking about her and having felt her skin on mine was making me feel tingles in my entire body, something that never happened before.

She pushed a lock of her hair behind her ear, smiling gently, and it was one of the most beautiful smiles in the world. It was like she didn't have all the problems plaguing her life anymore. Her son, her mother, and her job. I knew more about her life than I wanted to admit publicly.

"Thank you. I thought I was going to fall and everybody would be laughing." She peeked over my shoulder again. "Well, everybody was laughing, but not anymore. It's like..."

"They don't really see you? I think that's true, but it's not so for everyone." And I snuck that in without feeling a shred of shame. It wasn't the first time I was picking up a girl, even though this was happening naturally. I didn't come here thinking that I was going to score. Rather, it just happened automatically.

One moment she was just standing there after Aksa left and the next that asshole was riding fast on his motorcycle, and then the next she was with her clothes all wet.

Although, I couldn't help but deny that it kind of looked good – the way that her clothes were wet, that was. She was already curvy before and now she was even more so, her clothes clinging to her body, and I could even see the outline of her pair of panties. Lacy. I liked it, though that wasn't something I would ever bring up. Right now, the only thing she wanted to do was to get away from here as soon as possible, something that I could relate to.

"Yeah, pretty much nobody there even glanced at me once. I was like a ghost in there," she said.

"It was pretty much the same way for me."

She gave my shoulder a gentle punch, smiling. "No way. Everybody over there was sucking up to you."

And I supposed it was a good thing that at least my wife wasn't coming down here. I was alone, pretty much, as I should be. Although, there was no denying that she could be coming down any second now and I wouldn't be able to stop her.

She would ruin this nice, perfect moment with Antez, something I wasn't looking forward to. And it seemed that Antez wasn't going anywhere, either. She was staying with me, and that allowed me to do something I thought I never would.

"You weren't paying enough attention. Nobody wanted to talk to me, either," I joked, pointing with my eyes to the motorcycle that was parked in front of the building. "Wanna go with me somewhere else, where you don't have to even think about those people?"

She blinked twice. "Like where?" She asked, shifting her weight. It didn't mean that she was feeling nervous about this and about me, or did it? I didn't know, but I hoped she wasn't. Was I planning on taking this to another level or something like that? I didn't know, but I wasn't planning on doing anything specific.

This was just that other side of me speaking louder than usual. I just liked being nice sometimes, even though it wasn't a part of my more dominant personality.

She glanced behind her shoulder, finding my motorcycle. The look of disgust that dawned on her face was almost palpable, and I didn't know what to do, knowing that. Was she going to say no? Was she going to say that she now hated motorcycles so much she couldn't even go with me anywhere?

I didn't know, but something that was a first for me was also happening at this moment. My heart was speeding up and feeling tighter and heavier. Was I feeling nervous about this as well? Was I thinking about fucking her? So many questions, but I didn't have the answers to them.

"As long as you are a better driver than that asshole that splashed water on me," she joked, but she put her hand on her waist, showing me that she was actually considering that.

I didn't think she was going to. After all, the look of disgust on her face showed me as much.

"I promise you that I can look at what's in front of me, at least," I joked and she went along with it. She started walking to the motorcycle, waiting until I climbed on it. When I was with my hands gripping the handlebars, she climbed on the motorcycle behind me.

She put her arms around me, and I could feel the heat of her body pulsing, making me feel slightly warmer.

I looked behind my shoulder, wondering if my wife was going to show up, but for now, she was still inside the building, most likely chatting loudly and endlessly with the guests, and making new friends, too.

Since we weren't in love anymore, I knew she was having a great time there, most likely even considering possible candidates that would replace me.

It wouldn't be the first time that happened, I thought, turning on the motorcycle and hearing the engine as it roared to life. It was a beautiful, efficient engine, and it could make the motorcycle ride so fast it would be impossible to catch up to it.

Antez looked over my shoulder and made me check the building where the party was taking place again. That was when I noticed my wife kissing another guy, something that made me feel surer about this.

If she was having fun with another man, then I could do the same but with another woman. Someone better. Someone that made me feel different.

Again, it wasn't love or anything of the sort. It was just what it was. This was about me having a good time with Antez, who was looking more than willing to keep going with me.

I made the engine of the motorcycle roar several times and then I took off with her sitting behind me. When I did that, she tightened her arms on me, making me feel the beating of her heart behind me - or was that only me imagining things?

I didn't know, but I was still thinking, still enjoying this moment, and I just wanted to keep going.

Moments later, we were cruising across the city and it was great. She had her helmet on as did I. I wasn't going to do anything that could put her and me in danger. I wasn't that stupid and that was something I tried to instigate in my motorcycle club as well. I always told my mates that every time we rode, we had to take all the necessary safety measures.

Riding across the city on my motorcycle was something I would never forget, and I was sure that Antez was feeling the same way, even though she was slightly afraid of it. I could also feel how wet her clothes were, something that made me want to buy her new ones. And even though I could, I didn't want her to think that I was being so nice that the only thing I was thinking about right now was how I was going to get between her legs.

Then, we finally reached my place. It was a large house located on the outskirts of the city, and it overlooked it, providing me with one of the most amazing views in it. Just looking at it was breathtaking, even though it was dark and there wasn't much of a moon to speak of in the sky.

But that was just a detail. Antez was with me, things were beginning to get hot, and she climbed off the bike without a fuss.

What was going on in her mind right now?

CHAPTER 5

Antez

So, what was I thinking, following him to his house? It was nice, but there was no denying that I was doing something crazy. Not to mention that I was pretty sure Aksa would at some point be waiting for me or would be looking for me at the party, but I wasn't going to be there.

And that was for the better. I wasn't sure what I was thinking, going there to that party, trying to mingle with people so different from me. At least I was here with someone that for sure wasn't... He was actually different from me, too, wasn't he?

A biker. A billionaire. So many things about him showed me he was so different from me, and yet he took me to his home and was being nice to me. He was actually understanding me, being just in front of me as he opened the door.

I wasn't going to deny that his house, which was more like a mansion, was big. It wasn't just that, too, but also breathtaking. The first moment I stepped inside it, I was completely unsure about what I should do. His living room alone was bigger than my whole apartment, which wasn't saying much, I had to admit.

And the worst thing about this? The one that was nagging me the most? It was knowing that this was natural to him. He wasn't even remotely shocked by the quality of his house. He shouldn't be, after all. This was far from the first time he was here.

What was really going to happen here? I didn't know. I

supposed I had felt so much stress with my friend at her party that I was enjoying this moment much more than I should be.

It was just really so good.

"Quite a difference, isn't it? Just being away from that party and being where there aren't so many people around," He said, smiling as he went to the kitchen, which was adjacent to the living room. It was actually just one big, impressive room.

I walked until I was behind the kitchen island. He went down somewhere in the basement and then came back holding a wine bottle in his hand. I didn't know much about wines, but from the looks of it and considering that it was probably in his wine cellar, it meant that it had to be old and that it was stored there for a long time.

I wasn't someone that drank a lot, but I always had a soft spot for wines, especially the ones that were rare or were of high quality.

He put the wine bottle on the kitchen island, reached out behind him for a corkscrew, and then he opened the bottle. The moment he did that, I already felt some of the smell coming from it, and it was excellent. It even made me close my eyes slightly, just cherishing the smell for what it was.

"What wine is that? It's so good," I asked and he smiled, and I noticed the way, firm and confident, that he was holding the wine bottle. I didn't know why I was noticing that, just hoping that I wasn't beginning to develop feelings for him that I shouldn't. After all, I was just enjoying tonight for what it was, just pretending that it was as good as I thought it was going to be, like when I accepted my friend's invitation to the party. If only I had known then that it was going to be such a drag.

"It's… I don't think it matters, do you? Just the smell should be showing you how good it is. Plus, I would be lying if I said that I know much about wines." He smiled again and I watched with the utmost attention the way he stretched his lips.

I was focusing so much on his lips and his teeth that I didn't even know what I was doing and how pathetic I was probably looking to him. I mean, I was doing my best to not show that there was some connection forming between us, but it was so difficult not to do that, especially when just looking at him was making me feel some heat forming between my legs.

"Well, I don't think so," I said when he reached inside one of the cabinets on the wall and he got two wine glasses. I had come from the party after drinking – just a little, though. I couldn't drink here as much as I wanted and without getting drunk. I knew my limits, after all.

It would be a pity and a shame to not at least take a couple of sips from that wine. The color and the smell were great. They made my stomach rumble as though I was hungry, and I wasn't. If there was at least one good thing about that party, it was the food. I managed to eat so much while I was there.

He poured some of the wine into one glass and then he handed it to me. I was holding it in my hands, moving it left and right in circular motions as I looked at his eyes and noticed that they were so different from the eyes I would have thought a biker like him had.

He poured himself some wine and was also looking at me from behind his glass. I didn't know what he was thinking, but he was still smiling softly, still showing me his perfect teeth. I never thought that a biker like him had such shining teeth, but that was what I was seeing right now, and just looking at his lips was making me want to kiss him.

I shouldn't be feeling this way. I shouldn't be feeling attracted to another man. I knew how dangerous that was after breaking up with my ex.

I took a sip of the wine and asked, "So, how is it? Good enough for you?" He asked, clearly mentioning the wine, but for a moment I thought he was talking about something else.

For now, it was good that we were both separated by the kitchen island. I felt a little safer, knowing that he couldn't just reach over and grab me.

"It's good. It's really good," I said after taking another sip from the wine glass, putting it down so that I could better admire what was around me.

I wasn't going to deny that it wasn't just the man that was making me feel things I shouldn't be. Even though I wasn't someone that liked cooking often, there was no denying I could imagine myself spending hours baking something in this kitchen. But knowing my life, who I was, and the fact that I was stuck in my dead-end job... I knew that would never happen.

That was why I was keeping my expectations low. It could be that tonight was going to end with a one-night stand, but it wasn't going to be much more than that.

We continued to sip from the wine until we were a little tired and we wanted to do something else. What was that something else going to be? I didn't know, but I was going to leave that up to the motorcyclist.

Perhaps he was going to show me something about his life, something that I thought wasn't a part of it. So, I knew that he liked his wines as much as he liked his motorcycles, but there were still so many things about his life I had no idea about.

What about his brother? Father? Mother? I didn't know anything about them.

I didn't work for his company and he wasn't my boss, but he was associated with the company that I worked for. He was always there, always crossing the main room where all the desks and employees were, and I always had some chances to steal some glances at him.

I never did that when I was still with my ex, but ever since I broke up with him and I started to feel better, things changed. I started to look at Harry with different eyes.

CHAPTER 6

Harry

What was even happening here? One moment she was asking me so many questions about my life, and I was just pouring everything out, telling Antez everything about my life. She was stunning, sitting beside me on the couch while we tried to watch whatever was on the screen of the TV. It was displaying something, but I couldn't focus on it. My eyes were focused on Antez, on her body, and on how stunning she was. I just couldn't stop looking at her as though we were going to start to kiss, but I knew that wasn't going to happen.

After all, just across from us, above the TV, was my portrait with my wife, showing me and her together, at our wedding. It reminded me of a good time, when I thought we had a good thing going on between us, that we were actually in love, but that was actually in the past. Now, I knew that my wife was still kissing that other guy at the party and she wasn't ashamed of it.

Tonight, she would come back and pretend that it didn't happen, even though, when she lied down in the bed by my side, I would feel his smell coming from her, and that would infuriate me. I would feel so much hatred I would start to imagine myself choking her until she died.

That was why this moment was so good. It allowed me to not be thinking about anything that wasn't how stunning and how sweet Antez was. She was with her hands on her lap, looking at me after she asked me so many questions about my life. It was like an interrogation, but I knew that she was just learning everything about me she could.

And at some point, she mentioned that she thought my wife was a good person. She had a high opinion of her, something I didn't think possible. I hated my wife so much right now that I thought nobody could ever have such an opinion of her.

Much less Antez, the woman sitting by my side and whose warmth I could feel, calming me down. There were always so many shitty things going on in my life that I just wanted to pretend that I wasn't stuck in a marriage that didn't make me happy anymore.

"I'm so sorry for you. I'm so sorry that she doesn't value you for the man you are," she said and that was something I never thought I would hear from her. I never thought that anyone would say something like that to me without making me feel wrong about it, but the truth was that Antez was being nice to me, was being understanding, and she spent hours here with me, sitting on the couch, one movie after the other, just listening to everything I had to say, and I had a lot to say.

I supposed that was one of the reasons why I was a biker. That was what I wanted to be so that I could let out my rebellious side.

This was happening a lot quicker than I thought. "I'm happy you think that way," I said, putting my arm around her and she let it happen. For a moment, I thought she would just stand up in a heartbeat, looking at me wide-eyed, shooting me accusation after accusation, saying that I was taking advantage of her or something like that.

But the truth was, after being reminded that my wife was cheating on me and didn't at all feel bad about it, I just wanted this whole thing to be over.

That was why I was letting her lean over, our lips approaching, our breathing feeling caged, the warmth of her body, the smell of her perfume, and pretty much everything else overwhelming all of my senses.

And it was like fireworks exploded in my mind.

The moment our lips touched, it was like I couldn't stop feeling them. I was rubbing my lips on hers, enjoying this for much more than it was. Her lips were wet and hot. She was kissing me back and following my pace the way I wanted her to keep following.

No denying that this was far from the first time that Antez was kissing someone.

And this was good. I was still thinking about my wife, but also that I was getting one up on her. I wasn't going to be an asshole and let her find out about this, though.

I didn't even know where this was going, but the chemicals that it was releasing in my mind… It was almost too much. I couldn't help but feel like I needed more and more of Antez, and her body was just so warm, so curvy, so perfect, and I couldn't stop moving my fingers all over her curves, going as far as popping open the front of her dress.

And she gasped, her breathing not at all controlled right now. I didn't think that this was taking such a toll on her, but the fact was that it was. She was even sweaty too, and I couldn't help myself. I brushed my hand on her cheek, feeling her sweat, and I felt her skin and her warmth even better than I was already feeling.

Antez was looking into my eyes and I knew there were so many things she was telling me right now with that stare alone. It was as though she wanted this to continue but couldn't stop it anymore.

"Allow me," I said, putting my arms around her, lowering the top part of her dress, and then unsnapping her bra. Finally, my eyes could delight themselves in the perfection that was her breasts. Her bosom… To say that I was just feeling it with my hands right now would be an understatement, and it was like she was reading what I was thinking. She soon lied down on the couch and I was on top of her, my fingers exploring and pressing her breasts, loving the way she closed her eyes.

Alright, I had her where I wanted her to be, and I couldn't have enough of her breasts. Those nipples… so hard and perky, tempting me to pinch them, and I did that, groaning when my hand started to rip a section in the front of her dress.

I knew that I was ruining it, but it didn't matter. I was going to give her money to buy another that was even better than this one, and I was sure she was going to love it.

And the best thing about this was that she was giving everything she had to me. She didn't stop me when I started to remove her dress. I put it where it would not get in the way. My hands continued to explore her body, and I noticed that her pussy was begging for me to start to do wonderful things to it.

Glancing down, the first thing I noticed was that she was incredibly wet. It was like this was her first time having sex with a man, but I was sure that wasn't the case. I then moved my body down, putting my head right above her sex, and I started to lick her pussy over and over, quickly and then slowly, enjoying the feeling of her wetness on my tongue.

She dug her fingers into my backside and it was strong enough to rip the material of my coat. I felt and heard it being ripped, and then I had to take it off me, putting it where it would also not bother us.

I knew what Antez wanted more than anything else right now. She wanted to see my naked body, and I was going to give her exactly that. Without even thinking about it, I pushed myself up, taking off my shirt as well. I didn't even know how I managed to put it on so that I could go to the party, but the fact was that it happened and it was annoying.

I just felt so free right now without the coat and the shirt on. And in the meantime, I felt this urge to take off my pants, and I did exactly that only a couple of moments later and after getting off the couch so that I could do that more easily. As soon as I did that, I climbed back on the couch and put myself right on top of her.

Antez was looking at me wide-eyed and I knew that she wanted me to do what I was thinking. I wanted to go inside of her, and that was exactly what I was going to do. Not thinking twice about it, I just put her legs over my shoulders and then I put a condom on my cock, covering it. I wasn't drunk or crazy enough to fuck her without protection, and I knew she appreciated that.

It was for that reason she didn't say anything when I just went inside of her, piercing her flesh, stretching her walls as wide as they could be stretched, and then going all the way inside of her, rolling my hips as soon as I noticed she was getting used to my size.

I noticed the way she was biting her bottom lip, wincing, and thus my pace was slow in the beginning. But it was only momentary. As soon as I noticed that she wasn't feeling as much pain, I increased it, and when I found my desired rhythm, I started to fuck her much more pleasantly, my balls slapping against her ass, and it was one of the most amazing moments of my life.

When I came, I knew I would never forget it.

CHAPTER 7

Antez

When I woke up, I knew I did something wrong. I promised myself I would never have sex with another man, but it just happened, and now I felt as though my world was going to fall apart. How the hell did this happen? I asked myself, noticing that I was looking at the ceiling and that Harry was lying on the floor, passed out, snoring, some lines of saliva coming from the sides of his mouth.

He looked handsome, and I wanted him to put his arms around me again, but I knew I made a mistake and I had to end it right at this moment. Without even thinking about it, I just stood up slowly, measuring the weight that my feet were touching on the floor of his house. Good thing that it was carpeted and I wasn't making much noise as I walked on it.

I was naked and I didn't even know how I was going to get out of his house, especially given that it was walled and I wouldn't be able to climb over the wall. Well, it wasn't like I had many options. I could either stay here in his house, wait for him to wake up, wake him up myself, or try to climb over the wall and hurt myself in the process.

I sighed, looking around and checking out his house again. It was just so modern, so neat, and everything was so clean. What was I even doing and thinking, though? Was I imagining myself living here? Was I thinking that he would adopt my son, that I would marry him, and that we would live happily together ever after?

Ridiculous. Pathetic. That would never happen.

The worst thing was that I didn't have any clothes I could use. Our sex was so wild and raw that he ripped my dress off my body. It was there, lying on the floor, divided into two pieces. Now that I was thinking about it, how did Harry even manage to cut my dress like that with his hand? It wasn't like it was bad or that the material was getting rotten or anything like that. He was just that strong, and he was so obsessed with our sex that he didn't even stop when he started to do that.

That was how much he wanted me, I thought, blushing.

The most logical thing would be to continue to wait until he woke up, and then he would take me to my apartment, where I would be able to put on new clothes, or he would do what he should do – in which case it was to buy me a new dress. After all, I paid a pretty penny for that one.

A pretty penny… I thought, lamenting the fact that that was it. That was my dress now, a piece of ripped cloth, and when I came back home, my mom would start to unload so many questions on me, asking me about what I was doing. After all, I told her I was going to be back home last night, but it was already the morning and the sun was beginning to rise over the houses.

Looking outside, I couldn't help but also imagine myself living in this neighborhood. It was so calm, so serene as though nothing bad could ever happen here. There were never any arguments, no families fighting, no disagreements, no nothing, and for my mental health alone that would be fantastic.

I took a deep breath in and I decided to do something even crazier than all the other options combined. I didn't know much about his house, but I knew that it had a second floor, where most likely his bedroom was. Without thinking twice about it, I made my way up there, measuring the way that I was walking on the floor and especially up the staircase.

In a moment, I was on the second floor, looking around and then finding a couple of doors down the hallway. I knew that one of them was going to take me to his bedroom, and I opened one door after the other, hoping that I was going to stumble inside his bedroom, but I didn't find it.

What the hell? I thought, my body covered with the towel I had found in one of the bathrooms on the first floor. I knew that this house was big, but I didn't think it was so big that I couldn't even find his bedroom even though I was actively looking for it.

Then, as if by sheer luck, after opening another door and realizing that I was lost on the second floor, I found his bedroom. Or at least, it looked like his bedroom. So many of the other rooms that I'd found were for the pianos or a couple of other things, most of them unnecessary for his house. But I supposed that they added some charm to it.

I found his closet, opened it, and then I took one of his pants and one of his shirts. I could just imagine what the guy from the taxi was going to be thinking about me when he looked at me, finding me in front of Harry's house, wearing clothes that even though they fitted me, were also too big for me.

Not to mention the neighbors most likely thinking that I was a criminal that had just robbed his house or something like that.

After all, so many things… Well, I would better not even say it.

A moment later, I found what I was looking for and now I was looking a little bit more decent. At least I could walk outside and get to the taxi. I just asked for a taxi to come over, and in less than a couple of minutes, it was going to be here.

But that left me with a big problem. How was I going to get out of the property where his house was without climbing over the wall? And how could I climb over the wall without hurting myself and looking like a fool when everybody was looking at me wide-eyed, wondering what the hell I was even doing? So many questions, but now that I just finished calling the taxi to come here, there was no time to be thinking about them anymore. It was time to leave this place, even though that was going to make Harry wonder about what I was feeling when I woke up.

I was planning on telling him, by texting him, exactly what I was thinking about our sex. I wasn't going to hurt him or anything like that. Not to mention that I was certain someone like him wouldn't feel bad if I said that I didn't want anything else to do with him.

I finished walking down the staircase and I could see that he was still lying on the floor, snoring and sleeping. Thank goodness. For a moment, I really thought that I was going to find Harry staring at me, glaring at me as though he was thinking about killing me.

His billionaire side would never change his biker side, after all, and more and more I knew that he was thinking about turning his MC into a member of the 1%. Would he do something like that, essentially turning him into a criminal that would never get caught because he was filthy rich?

I didn't know, but that was just another reason that I feared him so much right now – to the point that I was walking over to the door out of his house while weighing each of my footsteps, and that wasn't something easy to do. It was the opposite, in fact. It tired my body so much I was getting sweaty again – not a good thing when I entered the taxi, I thought.

And it had already come. Shit. That meant climbing over the wall right away. I didn't even remember how Harry had opened the front gate of the property. All I knew was that the taxi driver was honking and waiting for me.

I knew that I looked like a mess. My makeup was all undone, smeared on my face, and when I managed to climb over the wall – that was more like a big 'if' – he would burst out laughing when I fell on the sidewalk.

Well, it still looked like I didn't have much of a choice.

CHAPTER 8

Antez

I stood behind the wall after having told the taxi driver that I was going to have to climb over the gate. He was on the other side of the wall, saying that he was going to catch me when I fell. Easier said than done, but I couldn't imagine myself not doing this.

I explained to him a little bit of what was happening here, though a lot of it was filled with lies. I would never tell a stranger that I had come to a house, had sex with the host, and that now I couldn't leave.

"Come on, I'm going to help you down," he promised, and I tried climbing up, only to slip off, feel my body going down, and then, when I thought I was going to fall on the grass, a pair of hands grabbed me.

It was just like it happened that time. I looked over my shoulder, finding none other than Harry, who was half-dressed and most likely asking himself what the hell I thought I was doing. Even I was wondering that right now, feeling slightly happy that he didn't let me fall. I thought that, for sure, that was what was going to happen.

And now I was thinking that he had many questions for me.

"What's going on with you? Did you hurt yourself" The taxi driver asked, sounding worried, and here I was thinking that he was going to start laughing at me for being so pathetic.

"No, I've got her," Harry replied, standing in front of me and putting his fisted hands on his waist as though he was talking to a child and not a fully grown adult that had been through a lot of shit.

"Oh, thank goodness. I thought she was going to hurt herself. Are you the owner of the house? She was trapped and couldn't get out. Can you open the gate for her?" The driver asked, sounding more worried than before.

"Yeah, I'm going to get to it as soon as I'm done with something else," he said without taking his eyes off me. They were making me feel slightly uncomfortable. Harry was without his shirt and he wore only a pair of shorts.

His body, covered with tattoos, looked even more threatening right now, and also even more lust-inducing, making me feel that characteristic heat between my legs.

I walked with him a little far away from the gate, knowing that he wanted to talk to me about what happened, and there was a lot he wanted to say right now.

"Why were you trying to climb over the gate?" He asked, sighing. I could feel how disappointed he was in me, something I thought would never happen between me and Harry.

In the meantime, I was looking more embarrassed by the minute. I didn't even know what I was thinking when I did that. Could I phrase my answer without looking like an idiot? The more I thought about it, the more certain I was that it was impossible.

"I just didn't want to wake you up."

"Really? Because of something like that you were going to hurt yourself?" I lifted my hand, more than willing to say that things weren't exactly like that, but then he narrowed his eyes, stopping me before I said anything even more idiotic. "And you know that was going to happen if it weren't for me, again."

I blushed. How was I going to say that he was wrong? The truth was that he wasn't and I was jumping through hoops just so that I didn't have to talk to him.

Just so that things happened more discreetly... I didn't know what was going on in my mind right now, but it was making me feel like I was living in a nightmare. A nightmare where the sun shone brightly, the birds chirped in the trees, and a squirrel climbed one of the trunks.

What was even going on right now? Could I escape from this?

I sighed, admitting defeat. "Yes, you are right. I could have done that, but I just didn't want to talk to you. What happened last night…"

"You didn't like it?"

"No, it's not that. It's just that things are too complicated. You have your wife and I have my son, and I shouldn't be seen with another man. Not to mention that my ex could find out about this."

"If he does and threatens you, I'll be more than willing to put him back in his place and he'll know that he can't mess with you again," he promised, making me feel that no matter if he had ulterior motives or not, his intentions were genuine, and he wasn't lying when he said that.

He would put himself in danger to keep me safe from my ex, the man that I hated the most for all the lies, for beating me up, for doing things to me that I didn't even want to think about.

This was such a nightmare.

Did I think that a billionaire who thought that he was a biker was going to help me with that? That he was going to make everything better and that was that?

I didn't think so, and I just wanted to end what was going on here as soon as possible.

"Thank you for saying that, but I don't want any bloodshed or anything of the sort. I just want my life to have some peacefulness so that I can do my things and keep living it without having to think about anything that could disrupt that."

"That's fair, but…" He looked over my shoulder. "I think it's about time we finally opened the front gate," he said, and I followed him out of the property.

After he opened it, I was finally outside of the place and the taxi driver was looking at me wide-eyed. He just couldn't wrap his head around what happened.

One moment I was with Harry, we were having this short argument, and then the next I was finally walking outside of the property as though nothing happened.

He was in the right to be feeling confused right now.

I glanced at Harry, who wasn't looking at all ashamed that he was almost naked outside of his house. Not even the taxi driver was looking at him with curious and judging eyes. He wasn't surprised by this at all. I supposed that him being a driver meant that he had seen so many worse things before in his life.

"I can pay the fare for you if you want," Harry offered and I shook my head, waving my hand.

"No need for that. I have enough money with me," I said and opened the door of the taxi, sitting down in it. When I was finally inside the taxi, I felt so much more relieved. It was like I was finally outside of his sphere of influence and that he couldn't change my thoughts or make me more malleable.

Harry didn't say anything, just putting his hands in his pockets and turning around, leaving. I watched him as he entered his house and disappeared. I didn't have much time to wonder where he was going exactly.

In a moment, the taxi driver was already entering the next road and I was left alone, even though the driver was in front of me, steering the taxi as he started to hum.

It was like he could read what I was thinking. His humming was comforting and it allowed me to think better, and reflect back on what happened. I shouldn't have acted based on my emotions and I shouldn't have had sex with Harry. In fact, I should've stayed right where I was, doing nothing, just pretending, that when I fell, it didn't actually happen. I should have thought that this was going to happen. I should have realized that I was feeling exposed and vulnerable.

It was good what we had, though.

Minutes later, I finally stepped outside of the taxi, finding none other than my mother coming out of the apartment building, running over to me with her arms spread out wide.

"Antez, what were you thinking, disappearing like that from

the party without saying anything? Me and Aksa and everyone else were so worried about you!" She shouted, but it wasn't true.

I didn't think that Aksa was worried. Mom might have been, but she was different. She was a little... difficult to understand sometimes. Sometimes she was her normal self.

Other times, she was a little out of herself, more often than not mumbling something unintelligible.

Thinking that, I still couldn't help but smile when I noticed my son running over to me, his arms spread out wide, his smile going from ear to ear.

He was the only good thing that my ex left to me.

CHAPTER 9

Antez

It was raining outside, or more like the rain was pouring in the city, pelting it. I was pretty sure that, stepping outside, I would drench my clothes completely and wouldn't be able to dry them without a clothes dryer, an item that I couldn't buy yet.

That meant hanging my clothes in the apartment, which was too small and certainly not fit for that. We didn't have a balcony, after all.

Just glancing down, seeing how high up I would be, would make me feel dizzy, too. I always looked down, always thinking about what would happen if I just... fell off the balcony, going down, speed increasing, the wind on my face, the ground nearing me constantly, nothing stopping me, and no one to catch me.

Why was I thinking something so terrible right now? The truth was that I was supposed to get up and take the subway to work, but I couldn't. Just thinking about stepping outside in the rain, it hitting my face, wetting my clothes, ruining my makeup, and doing things even worse than those... I couldn't help but feel a little lost right now.

I had to go to work, though. If I called in sick, my boss would most likely think that something was off, and he would be right. I wasn't sick... or was I? My life was such a whirlwind of different things right now it was difficult to figure out what exactly was going on in my mind.

All I knew was that I couldn't continue like this, lying down in the bed, thinking, feeling something different in my belly but that I couldn't quite put my finger on.

It was a different feeling, but one that I was familiar with. And I looked down across the entire room and found something on the dresser that caught my attention.

A portrait of me and my son. Just the two of us, smiling, happy, on vacation right after I dumped my ex and he hid from the police. Thinking about him, I couldn't help but feel a knot in my stomach and start to remember everything that happened after my one-night stand with Harry.

How the fuck did that even happen? I knew how. I was vulnerable and felt exposed. He was nice. He asked me many questions, supported all of my decisions, dissed my ex for everything he did, and promised me that he would put him in his place if he showed his ugly smug here again.

He was a good man, but I knew that nothing would happen between us. I thought that he would come and say something about what happened that night, but he didn't. Silly me. He didn't even have me on any social media website or my phone number.

Of course that he wasn't going to call and say what he thought about it. Not to mention that I probably hurt his feelings by saying that I didn't even want to wake him up so that I didn't bother him.

That was such a mess, I thought, sitting up on the bed and looking around. My room was dark. Silly me. Of course it was dark. I didn't turn on the lights and was still feeling something funny in my stomach. I was beginning to grow suspicious about it, and kind of beginning to think that it could only mean one thing.

But how could that be, when Harry used a condom and I took the pill so there were no chances I would get pregnant? I didn't know, but that was my strongest suspicion right now. I had been in this situation before, or in another that was eerily similar.

I slid out of the bed and almost fell over, supporting my weight on the wall. Thank goodness that didn't happen. It was almost like something was forcing me to eventually fall once, at least, but that wasn't going to happen.

I took a deep breath in and started to go to the bathroom. I didn't have a bathroom connected to my bedroom. The bathroom was actually down the hallway between the bedrooms. That sucked, but there was nothing I could do about it.

I was just happy that we at least had a bathroom that we could use and didn't have to share it with other people. We had lived before in other places where we had to share the bathroom with some residents from other rooms, and that was a memory I wanted to forget. Actually, there were so many things I wanted to forget about, but that one was at the top of the list right now.

I eventually reached the bathroom when I felt something nasty and hot coming up in my throat, pouring it out when it was already too late. It was my dinner. Chicken, some rice, beans, and that sort of thing. Nothing that would make anyone think we were finally turning things around in my life.

I was happy that I managed to lift the lid of the toilet just in time. I thought I wasn't going to have enough time to do that, but I did and I felt some level of disgust, seeing that green goo or stuff or whatever it was called in the water of the toilet, making it look more tainted than it already was.

I was huffing when I was done with that, coming to a conclusion I didn't want to face. It could be that I was pregnant, but the last time I had sex, it was with Harry, and if I was indeed pregnant and the baby was his – and it was possible that it could be more than one – I didn't even want to imagine what would happen.

My throat was a little hurt and dirty after pouring out some of my dinner from last night into the toilet. I was still breathing with difficulty when it was over, and I was also happy that I didn't feel I was going to puke again, which was a big relief.

I just closed the lid of the toilet and then I flushed it when I noticed that someone was behind me. For a moment, I thought that he was a ghost, perhaps even my boyfriend, who might have died and had just come here to kill me, but it was just my son.

He was with his hand on the doorway, his body leaned against it, and he was looking at me with worried eyes. I didn't know what he was thinking, but he had to be concerned about my well-being.

I always told myself that it didn't matter how shitty my life was, I was always going to do the right thing. And keeping that in mind, I straightened up my spine and approached him before he asked, "Mommy, are you feeling okay?"

I nodded once and slowly, my hand on his shoulder and then leading him out of the bathroom. "Yes, mommy's feeling okay, but she ate something bad last night. I'm feeling better now, though."

I took him to his bedroom, dressed him for school, and then I took him outside. I was happy that my mom was already waiting for me there. She already had breakfast and did pretty much everything else she needed, except remembering that she was supposed to dress Khalan for school. I approached her with glaring, judging eyes, and she shrugged her shoulders, waving her hand.

She knew what she did, but for the time being, she was going to pretend she didn't.

"Sometimes, I forget some things," she said, taking his hand and then going with him where the bus was going to stop. It was a bus that took the students to their schools. It was yellow and old, and kind of familiar, too.

"Try not to forget about that sometimes," I said and she shrugged again, but I was happy that at least she was going where she needed to go now. She stopped with my son just under the bus stop, and at least she had an umbrella. That meant they weren't going to get drenched by the rain, something that already made me feel less concerned about Khalan.

So, he was going to be okay. I just got him dressed, gave him breakfast, he wasn't hungry, he was well, he wasn't hot, wasn't cold, and he looked ready for the classes, and I was certain that he wasn't going to get bullied or anything of the sort.

He was going to be fine at school, too. Why was I feeling so worried?

CHAPTER 10

Antez

So, it happened and I didn't know what to do. I was in the hospital. I was in the operating room after finding out that my baby was already coming. I was holding her in my arms. It was a baby girl, and she was pretty. She looked like Harry, but that couldn't be. I was just imagining things. Except that 'imagining things' didn't make any sense.

That was a shitty excuse for what happened. I should own up to it and say to myself that I committed one of the worst mistakes of my life after having that one-night stand with Harry.

And I was making it worse by not telling him about it. The moment I found out I was pregnant, my mom shot me question after question, cornering me against a wall, trying everything she could to make me spill out what happened, but even though I told her part of the truth, I kept the rest hidden. Why? It was simple.

Even if Harry was the father of the baby – and the more I was thinking about this, the more I knew he was – I was certain that he would sue me and destroy my life. Even though he tried to look more amicable when he was with me, showing me that he cared about me, and being the person I always wanted to spend the rest of my life with, the first thing he would think was that I used him for a baby.

He would think that I was using the baby so that I could fleece him.

And I could just imagine the shitstorm that would happen after that. His wife would find out about it, she would start to scream at me, and I would slap her face so that she stopped doing that.

And that was without mentioning how different I was from Harry. He was rich and tried to pose as a biker. We didn't have much in common other than the fact that we felt something for each other that was a lot more than just physical attraction.

After all, when I shared so much about my life with him, he showed me how much he cared, and I felt... Something similar to love.

It was still difficult to put it into words, but I felt his care, how protective he was, and his promises to keep me safe no matter what... I would never forget them.

That was why I was crying. Tears were coming out and rolling down my cheeks and I was certain that my mom was going to come into the room, barging through the door, and shoot me question after question about how I got pregnant. And I would tell her about Harry and she would flip out.

I could just imagine that happening. She always thought that he was a good match for me, but she didn't know how mistaken she was. Her whole life, she was always running after the wrong guy, and I was certain that Harry was another wrong guy – for me, at least.

After having my adventure with my ex, the only thing I wanted right now was a more stable man, and Harry was anything but stable. He was rich, the CEO of his company and yet he wanted to be a biker, to go out and ride with his buddies, pretend that he was a criminal, wear helmets, race on his motorcycle, and do things that I didn't even want to put into words right now.

Not to mention that I wondered about the kind of life that I would have with him. He wouldn't be around often for the baby. There were so many reasons not to tell him about the baby and the more I was thinking about it, the more I didn't want to do it.

That was why I was feeling so stuck where I was, holding the baby in my arms and feeling some tears coming out and rolling down my cheeks.

And I was just thinking about what my life was going to be like from now on when my mother entered the room. I thought she was going to barge through the door and start shooting me question after question, cornering me against the wall to argue about what happened, but she actually looked as though she could understand me.

She pulled a chair and sat on it. She put her hands between her legs, leaning over slightly so that she was looking more carefully at me and the baby. "I don't know what to say."

That was almost fine if I also didn't know what to say. But for the time being, I just hoped that nobody was going to say anything. "I don't think I want to talk about anything right now, mom."

"You are right to be feeling confused about this, but if there's something you need to tell me, then it's whoever the father of this baby is." This time, she was looking much more determinedly at my eyes, as though she was trying to read what I was thinking, but that wasn't so easy.

I just looked away and out, seeing the environment outside of the room. I wanted to be out there, to be walking in the garden in front of the hospital, to be contemplating the birds, the squirrels, the people going here and there, and even the cars as they drove to their destinations.

There was just something about not having to think that was tempting. I just didn't want to be thinking about my life.

"I'm not leaving this room until you tell me who the father of the baby is, and I do really believe that's the least I deserve to know about her," she said, lifting her finger and pointing it at my daughter.

I took a deep breath, feeling a little worried when I felt my daughter squirming slightly in my arms. She started to cry a little, but it was brief. I thought that she was going to begin to cry more loudly than that, but she behaved – this time, at least.

There were so many things about Ireena I didn't know about, and I just wanted to make sure that she was feeling okay. It could be that she was the kind of child that was loud and cried a lot, and I was just hoping that she was much more well-behaved than that.

I shook my head and caved in. "It's Harry." There, it was said and I couldn't go back on it. Now my mom knew who the father of the baby was, and she could do with that information whatever she wanted.

As soon as her mind finished processing it, she stood up slowly, putting her hand on her forehead.

She knew the implications of the truth, and she didn't want to face them. But she didn't have to. I was an adult and it was my fault that I let it happen.

"And this whole time, you've been keeping the pregnancy hidden from him. He's going to snap when he finds out."

"I'm trying to make it so he doesn't," I said, brushing my fingers over my daughter's forehead. Looking at her face was the only thing keeping me sane right now. That and also Khalan, my son.

"It's not that simple. Eventually, he's going to figure out something is different about you, especially now that you're going to have to miss some days of work to look after your daughter."

I took a deep breath in, shaking my head.

I knew that my mom was right about everything she was saying to me, but I just didn't want to face the truth. It was more difficult than I thought. Just thinking about it was making my heart feel tight, too.

She turned around, facing me with determined eyes. "You need to tell him everything or else I'm going to."

I bulged my eyes out. I knew that my mom was the kind of person that could do some crazy things when she was determined and obsessed, but I didn't think that she was going to start to threaten me like that.

"No, mom! You aren't going to tell him anything! Not yet, please. Give me some time. There's so much going on in my mind right now, so much to think about, and I just want to be with Ireena until I figure everything out."

She walked to the door, opened it, and then she stepped

outside into the hallway. And just before she left, she said, "I'm going to give you a couple of days to sort out your shit, but no more than that. I'm worried about Ireena as well and I just want to make sure that what happened between you, your boyfriend, and Khalan isn't going to come to pass again."

She closed the door, leaving me alone and with my thoughts.

She was right and some days from now I would call Harry to tell him everything. I knew that he would eventually find out the truth and it was better that he heard it from me.

CHAPTER 11

Harry

I was home, thinking, remembering my one-night stand with Antez. One of the most striking women in the world. Since then, she never talked to me. I knew that something wrong was going on here, but I couldn't put my finger on it. I thought that, by now, she would have already called me to say she felt sorry about it.

So far, though, that hadn't been the case.

Well, I couldn't just stay here in my house thinking about it and hoping that she was going to call me. Not to mention that the day outside wasn't helping me with my mood, either.

It was raining. A lot. The rain was pelting the city and I felt as though it would never stop. I thought that I would be able to go out today with my mates, but that wasn't possible.

I had been planning on going out with them, knocking back a few, getting to know some people, and riding across the city with them, but all our plans were thrown out the window the moment we noticed the heavy, stormy clouds in the distance.

Now, the only thing I could do was to keep looking outside, watching as the rain soaked the front yard. That and also reminisce every little thing that happened between Antez and me that night.

I could still remember the feeling of the touch of her fingers on me, her lips on me, her mouth breathing on mine, and everything else about her body.

But it was also much more than that.

I had always had a thing for Antez and I couldn't forget her.

I felt that what happened between us didn't end. It shouldn't have happened the way it did, with her trying to escape my house as though she was a prisoner.

Thinking about that wasn't going to help me right now, though. I did have her phone number. One of her friends told me what it was, and it was in the contact list on my phone, and I could call her and ask her about what happened.

I could ask her everything she thought about me since then, but that wouldn't be easy.

I could just imagine the avalanche of feelings and thoughts that would sprout up in my mind after I made that call, and I wasn't ready for that.

Looking outside, watching the rain as it pelted the city was calm and comforting, though.

But it wasn't enough. I still felt my heart tight as if something bad had happened or something worse was going to put my life at risk.

She knew so much about me and I knew so much about her. We didn't really know each other the way I thought it was going to happen, but she still knew enough about me and looking around me, I couldn't help but feel that my house was empty.

Without my wife, who just left me for the guy she was kissing at the party, it was and it felt empty. It was like I could feel the walls encroaching around me, trapping me in this place.

I shouldn't even be feeling that it was terrible to be in my house, but that was exactly how I was feeling right now. My house was like a mansion and it was big and spacious and it had everything I wanted, but without someone to fill the void that I felt by just being in this place, then it was pointless.

There was something I could do to help pass the time and that was to clean up my motorcycle. It was already clean, but there was nothing wrong with making it look even shinier than it was.

Without thinking twice about it, I just made my way to the

garage, opened the door, and then I found myself in the familiarity that it provided me with.

Being in the garage was stress-relieving.

I took all the things I was going to need, which were in a small metallic box, and then I went down on one knee by the side of my motorcycle. I spread some specialty cream wax on the tank cover, moving my hand on it, and wasn't thinking about anything in particular. Just being with my motorcycle was washing away my worries.

Everything was going great when I heard my phone buzzing and I noticed that it wasn't in the pocket of my pants.

My mind was such a mess that I must have left it somewhere else. I groaned, standing up, and then I turned after leaving the metallic box opened. I was going to continue applying the wax on my motorcycle later.

I made my way to the living room, finding my phone just on top of the fireplace. I picked it up and then my heart skipped a beat when I read a number on the screen.

It was Antez, no doubt. She was calling me and I didn't know how to react to that.

Why was she calling me right now after everything that happened and after not even talking to me, always avoiding me whenever I was at the company where she worked?

I didn't know, but this was the opportunity I was waiting for. This whole time, I had always been waiting for her to call me. I knew that she also had my phone number. One of her friends told me she asked her to give it to her, and I knew she could call me anytime she wanted.

Now that she was, I was feeling more certain about this. Even though it was difficult to start to think that she was going to say she was sorry about the way things happened, that was what I was hoping for.

I pressed my finger on the button, putting my phone next to my ear.

"Antez, I never thought you would call me," I said and I noticed that my voice was throaty, showing how emotional I was feeling right now.

The thing was, even though we didn't spend so much time together, there was still so much right about her, so much that resonated with me, and I wanted to capture those feelings again, to be with her, to see her in front of me, and to kiss her sweet lips.

"Harry, I don't even know how to start this," she confessed and I noticed she was going through something hurtful. I just wanted to be by her side so that I was comforting her, noticing that.

"What happened?" I asked, starting to pace in the room. Not even the loud rain outside could make me less focused on the call right now.

"You need to come here to my apartment, and please... Don't hate me."

Hate her? I didn't know what she was talking about, but it didn't matter. It didn't matter what she said, but I just could never hate her for anything she did. Not to mention that she sounded so hurt I just could never and would never do anything that suggested I felt that way about her.

"I don't know what happened, but I'm going to your apartment, and I promise you that I'm not going to hate you," I said and without thinking twice about it, I just hopped into my car, fired up the engine, and then I blasted my way to her apartment as fast as I could without breaking any of the traffic laws.

I was already outside her apartment a couple minutes later. It would have taken me much more time if I wasn't in a hurry. Her mother was the one that came to open the door for me, and then some seconds later, I was outside her bedroom.

She was in the bed, her eyes looking so deep, reddish, and hurt I immediately sat on the side of her.

"What happened?" I asked, wishing that I could hold her mouth, but we weren't that intimate – not yet, anyway. Now that she just called me and begged for me to come here, I was hoping that we were going to begin anew.

After all, without my wife being a thorn in my side, there were so many things I could do with Antez, and that thought alone was enough to make me feel so much more relieved.

"I don't even know how to do this. So much happened and so much of it was my fault. It's going to be difficult, but you have to forgive me for the mistakes I made."

And then she told me everything. She told me about our baby, that she kept it hidden from me because she didn't want me to find out, that she was afraid of what I would think if I knew about it, and even though those were facts I would never forget, only one of them stuck with me and it was that I had a daughter now.

I just never thought that I would, one day, become a dad.

CHAPTER 12

Harry

"Everyone, there's something I want to show you and tell you, and I know that you aren't going to like it, but we need to do this. You know The Night Outlaws, right?" I asked, stepping from side to side on the raised platform where I was.

My brothers were with me and they were going to help me.

I knew that this was unusual, but it felt much better than to be managing my company. I felt like I was where I belonged, where I was meant to be, and doing everything I wanted.

Even though… This was difficult.

It was my daughter's life that was on the line, and I needed to make sure that she was going to be safe.

The Night Outlaws hated me so much that they even kidnapped my daughter.

They took her from her mother, and now she was desperate, crying night after night in her bedroom. She didn't even have the strength anymore to get up and go to work, which only made this more desperate than it already was.

I supposed that I could call the police and ask them to do their job, but that wasn't a good solution. The problem was that the police were actually in on this.

The police hated me and my motorcycle club. We were called the Burnt Rodents. A silly name, but it was what it was. When

I picked that name for my motorcycle club, I didn't give it much thought.

I just picked whatever name I was comfortable with, and my brothers were also okay with it.

But that was something from the past, and now my mind was much more focused on something else.

It was going to be difficult. I knew that we didn't have much time. It was my daughter's life that was on the line, after all, and I needed to save her before it was too late.

We were going to raid the headquarters of The Night Outlaws, and it wasn't going to be easy. This whole time, I thought I was pretending to be a biker, but now I realized that I truly was one.

And not only that, but also a member of the 1% of motorcycle clubs in the country that were criminals.

This meant that the police were going to start to come after me, and I just couldn't imagine myself dealing with something like that without feeling a shiver of fear in my heart.

It was going to be so difficult that I knew my life was forever going to be changed. After all, the police were always keeping a blind eye on what I did in my free time, always keeping in mind that I was the CEO of my company and that they couldn't go after me so easily.

But now, things were different and I was unhinged.

I was going to raid the headquarters of The Night Outlaws, there was going to be a shootout, it was going to be bloody, and I had no idea if I was even going to come out alive after this.

The truth was that this was the first time I was doing this and it was more dangerous than anything else I did.

But my guys were roaring with me, throwing their hands up, clapping and cheering, and showing me their support as much as they could.

It was one of the few moments in my life where I felt I wasn't alone.

And with that in mind, I stepped down from the raised platform.

They started to pat me on the shoulders, shake my hands, and take me out of the warehouse where we were. It was our preferred meeting spot and I was thinking, now that I was probably going to step down as the CEO of my company, this place was probably going to become the address for my motorcycle club.

The physical address for it, to be more precise. I already had a digital address where anyone could fill up a form, showing their interest to join the motorcycle club, but that wasn't enough and it was only temporary.

Things were going to be so much more difficult from now on. With the police focusing more on me than ever before, it was going to be hard to keep myself away from their grasp.

They would never lock me up or any of my brothers, though.

That was why I had already included some judges and other justice system officials on my payroll. *In case* they tried to lock me up or even shut down The Burnt Rodents, it just wouldn't work.

I was ready to do anything possible so that it never happened.

I took a deep breath in, climbed up on my motorcycle, put on my helmet, and then I fired up the engine, blasting where the headquarters of The Night Outlaws were located.

I was certain that they were thinking I would never show up, even though this was my daughter's life that was on the line.

That was the way they were.

I didn't know the leader of The Night Outlaws personally, but I wasn't thinking about going there to start a conversation, regardless. Was it possible that the way out of this could be diplomacy? Sure, but right now, I wasn't thinking straight.

The truth was that I didn't feel like talking to anyone right now, much less the guy that kidnapped my daughter. If he thought that he could come out of this in one piece… Oh boy, he was going to be so disappointed.

As soon as I was with my daughter in my arms, I would find out who the leader was, and then I would ask him so many questions, and I would corner him against the wall so hard he would regret everything he did.

That was something I was promising myself, and I knew that it was going to happen the way I wanted it.

It was raining again, I noticed, getting off my motorcycle and taking my pistol from the waist holster.

Everyone that was in their headquarters started to come out, their footsteps showing how worried and afraid they were.

They also had guns, which they were pointing at me. Pistols and shotguns. Were they legal? I didn't know, but it wasn't like that mattered anyway.

What mattered was that everyone was coming out, and from among them was stepping who I was assuming to be their leader.

He was with my daughter in his arms, and he had a huge, victorious smile on his face.

I didn't know what he was planning on doing, but it wasn't going to work.

"Give me back my daughter or I'm going to kill your entire gang," I threatened, spitting saliva out of my mouth.

I didn't know if he was going to feel anything after my threat, but I was hoping that it was going to work.

Everything was said, I knew he knew this moment was going to happen, so he had to be planning something so that he could act accordingly.

"Harry Adams. You think that you are the president of a motorcycle club, but you are nothing more than a joke." And the moment he said that, I felt a muscle in my neck twitch. I wanted to kill him now more than anything, but I wasn't going to.

I wasn't even pointing my gun at him, even though that was something I should do. "But you can cool down now. I'm going to give you back your daughter after you promise me something, and knowing how good your word is and how important something like that is to people like us – bikers – then I know I'm not wasting my time right now."

I blinked twice. I had no idea what he was talking about, but he was curious and I just wanted to know what it was. After all, if there was a chance this could end in a way that didn't involve any bloodshed, then it was worth it – or was it?

I had to put the safety of my daughter first. Now that I was seeing her for the first time, the only thing I wanted to do was to make sure she was going to be okay.

She was crying, too. This had to end before it was too late.

He stepped toward me and now he was so close to me that I could feel the ice-cold breath coming out of his mouth. When was the last time that he brushed his teeth? I asked myself, realizing how inconsequential that was at the moment.

"Tell me what you are thinking, and I just might let you live," I threatened, and now he looked much more serious than before.

I didn't know who he was, but I knew he saw me as more than this – more than the president of a pet biker club. He was also talking to the owner of the company I was the CEO of, and that carried way more weight.

Still, this moment ending any differently than both of us killing each other was difficult, if not impossible.

ANTEZ' EPILOGUE

I was out of my bed in what felt like an eternity. I felt like I had been in my bed for days, weeks, and months, incapable of moving or going anywhere without my daughter. Her name... Ireena. It was a beautiful name and it took me so long to make sure it was the one that I wanted for her.

This was taking such a toll on me, and in the meantime, I just wanted to be holding my baby. Harry promised me that he was going to come back holding her in his arms, and I was waiting for him.

The problem was that he had blood in his eyes when he left, and since then I didn't know what he was going to do. Was he really going to go through with it? Was he really going to kill a lot of people just so that he made sure our baby was going to be okay? I didn't know, but I knew he wasn't the kind of man that made empty promises.

That was why I was waiting for him to come back. I knew he was going to be back no matter what. It didn't matter if there was going to be a shootout or anything of the sort where he was going, in the headquarters of the Night Outlaws, I still knew that he was going to be back with my baby in his arms.

It was his baby as well, and I felt so guilty for having hidden the pregnancy from him this whole time. I thought I was going to be braver about it, but that wasn't what happened.

In the meantime, my mom was with me and she was right behind me. She was with her hand on my shoulder, massaging it and comforting me as much as she could.

We didn't have the best of relationships, but she was the only person that could make me feel slightly better right now. Without this, I would be flipping out – or perhaps doing something worse than that.

"It's going to be okay. I know it's going to be okay because he is Harry and he cares about you. Plus, it really is his baby and he's going to do everything in his power to make sure that nothing happens to her."

I knew my mom was right, but it was still so difficult.

I took a deep breath in and turned around, just wishing to not be behind the window, looking out in the city, hoping that I was going to spot his motorcycle coming here fast in the distance.

And then, I noticed it. Or rather, I heard the noises. I heard the noises of the engines of the motorcycles coming in this direction, and I knew they were many.

It had to be Harry and the other members of his motorcycle club. I could see them on the freeway, and Harry had something in his arms. A small bundle. My little Ireena. Even though she was riding with her father on a motorcycle, a vehicle always dangerous to be riding on, she couldn't be any safer.

She couldn't be any safer because his arms provided her with safety and everything else she needed.

I knew that it was loud, that it was shaky, and the wind was blowing against her face, but she was still not crying. Even from a distance, I could see that she was behaving well and wasn't being fussy.

Thinking that, I just had to run down to the first floor of the building, where I knew I was going to see Harry climbing off the motorcycle and coming to see me.

When I was outside, he was already doing that and indeed was with Ireena in his arms. Tears were streaming on my cheeks. I was so overjoyed that I couldn't hide it, and even my mom and son were coming down here as well.

They were behind me, shocked by what they were witnessing.

"He really did it," my mom pointed out, but it was pointless to be doing that.

We all knew that he was going to come back with our baby in his arms, and now he was stepping toward me with her, and then he gave her to me. Finally, I was holding my baby in my arms again, and it was one of the happiest moments of my life.

I couldn't help but hug him tightly with my other arm, and then he turned with me, pointing toward the entrance to the building where my apartment was.

"We need to go up. My men are going to remain outside and keep the place protected. You can trust them as much as you can trust me," he said and I knew I could trust his words.

We went up to my bedroom, sat on the bed, and he brushed his fingers over my daughter's forehead, and I noticed that not even now she was being fussy and crying.

She was looking at her father with a lot of curiosity, wondering who he was and knowing that he was important. Someone special.

And looking at him, I knew that he had so much to explain to me after he left with his buddies. Did they kill everyone from The Night Outlaws MC? I didn't know, but I hoped that that wasn't the case.

HARRY'S EPILOGUE

This whole time, I thought that I was going to become a proper biker, but now I noticed that it wasn't what was going to happen anymore. The pregnancy changed everything, and since then we were getting to know each other better.

Antez. The most striking woman in the world, and I just couldn't spend a day without her.

Just being by her side was the most important thing in the world to me, and the only thing that allowed me to let go of the things I wanted to do, but which were actually hurting me.

She was holding the baby in her arms, and we were taking a stroll in the park. The park was located right across the street from the place where we now lived.

I also stepped down as the CEO of my company. I couldn't keep managing it and I didn't want to, anyway. There was just something about it that didn't resonate with me, and I didn't want to be bogged down in it, hoping that I would, one day, realize that it was important to me and that it actually made me happy.

That wasn't the case and it would never be.

I was just happy. We were living in Europe now. In France, to be more precise. There was just something about it that was special, that resonated profoundly with me, and I just couldn't spend a day without thinking how happy I was now that we were living here, away from everything going on in America.

The truth was that America was going down in a spiral of chaos and I didn't think it would ever return to normal. Was that even a possibility? I didn't know, but right now I just wanted to not be thinking about those things.

The park where we were taking a stroll was peaceful, and we could even hear the birds chirping in the trees. We knew that France wasn't doing particularly well in terms of so many things, too, but for the time being, there was something special about living here. Maybe it was the architecture, the people, the culture, or whatever, but here in this small city, we could do everything and we could have anything we wanted with a much better quality of life.

I knew how little this made sense, but it was just good not to be a biker anymore and not to think that someone was going to come for my life or to destroy my family.

The leader of The Night Outlaws… He was an asshole and I was certain that the police had already apprehended him and the rest of his motorcycle club.

I told them everything I knew, after all.

But right now, I was just so happy with myself that I couldn't even be bothered to even try to find out what truly happened to him. What happened in America didn't concern me anymore.

We stopped when we were next to a lake. It was so pretty, and we could see the light reflecting on the water's surface. We could also spot some people jogging in the distance, and little squirrels hiding in the trees.

Antez turned so that she was facing me, and I couldn't help but offer to hold Ireena in my arms.

"Thank you. I thought you were never going to ask," she said, giving me the baby, and I felt a lot better when I had her in my arms. When I first held her, I felt so clumsy I thought I was going to drop her, but thankfully that never happened and our baby was growing bigger and healthier by the day.

"It's nothing." I pointed with my chin to the bench in front of the lake, where we could sit. We had been walking in the park for a while now and I was already getting a little tired. It wasn't that I was sedentary or anything like that, but that I just wanted to relax a little bit. I wanted to be contemplating the lake and the area around it, the trees that surrounded it, and I knew I could do that and feel so much more comfortable. "Wanna go there?"

"Of course, my love." She said, giving my lips a peck. It wasn't the first time she called me her love. The first time that she said that to me, I didn't even know how to react. After losing my wife, I didn't think love was actually something that still existed. I actually thought that it was nothing more than a mirage or something that was told to me when I was little, but which was actually nothing more than a lie.

We sat down on the bench, and I was still holding Ireena in my arms. I could feel that she was getting a little fussy, moving her arms and legs about as if she was worried about something, and then I noticed that Antez was already offering me the baby bottle, which was in her shoulder bag before. We came prepared for our stroll in the park, and in case Ireena needed anything, she could have it.

I grabbed the baby bottle, put the teat between her lips, and I watched with joy as she started to suckle on it. For a moment, the only sound I could hear was the sound that her lips were making, suckling on the baby bottle's teat.

"She's so pretty," I said, brushing my fingers on her forehead and then looking at my wife, kissing her again.

Anyone looking at us would know that we were so deeply in love we knew that we could never be separated.

"I know, and I also know how much I love you," she said again and I could only say the same thing to her, kissing her one more time.

There was nothing better than to be with my wife in a place where I could think and do everything I wanted much more peacefully.

The End

Leave your review. Your feedback helps me improve immensely!

TEASER: HIS ACCIDENTAL TRIPLETS

BWWM Dark Mafia Romance

I could already feel the ogling of the customers, stepping into the main room of The Houz and hoping that I could get through the crowd as quickly as possible. But, looking at all these people standing in front of me, I could tell that doing that wasn't going to be simple.

I felt some tightness in my chest. It wasn't that I didn't like big crowds, but that this strip club, in particular, made me feel like ripping the flesh off my body.

I turned my head slightly to the right, finding a woman sashaying down the stage like she owned it. I couldn't help but feel a huge wave of repulsion, asking myself what she thought she was doing with her life.

I'd seen so many times what she did after The Houz closed. She went out to the alley in the back and allowed men to abuse her for some cash. I'd never say that I felt proud of my job, but at least I didn't have to do... the things she did for money.

My salary was just enough to survive, and I wouldn't say she was doing much better than I was. Quite the contrary, I was assuming. She probably made as much as I did, without the benefit of not having to sell out for some dollars.

If I could, I wouldn't be working here. I would be kicking back on the beach, sipping some coconut water, and making plans for the next luxury car I would buy.

I sighed, pushing through the crowd while holding a heavy bucket of water and a mop. I needed to reach the makeup room, or dressing room, or whatever it was called. In essence, it was where the 'performers' went to retouch their makeup and fix their hair.

Try as they might to look pretty, they couldn't change their souls. They sold them to the devil a long time ago. And while part of me blamed them for that, I knew that it wasn't that simple. Our failing economy and inflation were driving people to do the stupidest of things.

But that was enough rambling. I needed to keep pushing through this dancing, drinking crowd and reach that room. Upon getting there, I needed to make it look squeaky clean.

It wasn't that I thought I could really make that happen, though. The makeup room was usually dirty, and more often than not the girls that worked here took their clients there when they couldn't wait until they could find a more appropriate place.

Chicago had so many motels and yet people still had sex there. I didn't know what was usually going on in their minds, but it surely wasn't anything pretty.

Again, I pushed the rambling away and thought how ironic it was that a virgin woman like myself was working in a place like this. And being 21 now, with my parents having died a long time ago, I had to remember I wasn't in this situation because of my fault.

Or, maybe it kind of was. I was saving myself for the right man. So many of my friends – not the ones from church – kept insisting that I was making the wrong decision, that I was missing out, but they couldn't understand my motivations.

I grew up watching my mom and father being the happiest couple ever before they were killed, and they followed the same path I was.

A tear rolled down my cheek, remembering the day they died. My sister wasn't with me then, and I had to run back home to comfort her. Her crying made me break down too, and at that moment, I cried like a dam had burst.

Ever since then, I promised to keep Dalanie safe, and that's what I was doing. Even now, when she kept making it pretty clear she didn't like me one bit.

But she was only 17. I was pretty sure that, with time, she was going to realize I was the only thing standing between her and a life of complete misery, living in the streets and having to depend on other people to make ends meet.

Nevertheless, it wasn't like that was much different than what I was doing now, I thought with a frown.

I exhaled in pure relief when I finished pushing through the crowds and just when I thought I was safe, I felt something liquid and wet splashing on my shirt.

I snapped in the direction it came from, finding a white man in his early twenties with a grin on his face, holding a slightly-turned glass in his hand.

"You should be watching where you're going, ni-" he was saying before someone bumped into him, making his hand finish turning the glass until all of the beer in it splashed on my shirt.

On other occasions, when I was still starting out here, I would be fuming at what he did. But I'd be lying if I said this was the first time this was happening.

I shook my head, still holding the bucket with water in one hand and the mop in the other. I put the water bucket on the floor, rubbed my hand over my shirt in a futile attempt to dry the beer, and then turned and tuned that man out of my mind.

He was a racist jerk and, in this establishment, there were plenty of people like him. I needed their money to keep surviving in here, though, and it wouldn't be good for my boss if I insulted him, even though that idiot had almost called me the n-word.

I wasn't going to pretend it didn't bother me. It did – a lot, and I was already feeling my blood boiling. If I didn't need this job at all, I'd already be slapping the shit out of him and kicking him-

Oh God, what the hell was that thought that was crossing my mind now? I thought before opening the door of the dressing room and stepping into it.

Just not having to listen to the full volume of the music they played in the main room was very relieving. They played those kinds of shitty songs to keep their clients in some kind of haze in their minds, thinking about nothing but sex.

Alcohol and sex. What could really go wrong in a place like this?

As soon as my eyes scanned the room, I found what I was looking for. Some kind of weird goo on the floor, and it was probably the sperm of a man with a woman's bodily fluids mixed in it.

The thing itself made me feel a lot of repulsion, urging me to step out of this room right away. And it wasn't even empty either, I noticed, finding some girls standing not too far from me, talking among themselves.

In here, in The Houz, I was a nobody, and it wasn't like that would ever change. If anything, the women that worked here were going to keep thinking that way about me, looking down on me all the time.

I'd made a lot of noise, some water splashing out of the bucket when I walked into the room. And even then they didn't even turn their heads to me.

A lot of people would be feeling revolted at that, but not me. I actually kind of liked being treated as a ghost. I could come in and out of the strip club without anyone noticing me.

When walking outside, going to a supermarket to buy some groceries, and doing anything that didn't involve being here, I liked thinking that there was a pretty high chance nobody was going to recognize me.

I stepped to the goo on the floor, wondering if those women had been involved in the sexual matter that happened here not too long ago. My boss had called me to tell me I needed to wipe the floor clean right away.

He didn't really care what it looked and smelled like, only that he couldn't let a client potentially walk into the room, finding it in this condition.

But it wasn't like their minds would be able to process what had happened anyway, I thought with an uncomfortable, tight-lipped smile on my face.

I put the head of the mop into the water in the bucket, wetting it and then pulling it out. I rubbed it on the ground, right where that goo and stain were, hoping that it was going to be cleaned quickly.

I pulled the mop back, exhaling in annoyance as I found the goo and stain still right where they were. I had a dirty handkerchief put in one of the pockets of my pants, and I pulled it out as soon as I realized I was going to have to do some scrubbing.

Not really the ideal solution, but it was going to have to do. I wished we had some kind of cleaning product for situations like this, but as far as I knew, we didn't have any.

Getting on my knees, I couldn't stop my stomach from churning. The stench was so horrible it was making me wish I didn't have lungs.

I finished scrubbing the stain, already counting the minutes I could be out of here. I grabbed the mop, dried it somewhere outside the strip club, and then stashed it with the now-empty bucket of water in the cleaning equipment room.

I wasn't going to have to touch them until something-

I heard my phone buzzing in the pocket of my pants. My boss didn't say that I had to leave it in silence mode, and the music here in the dressing room was still loud enough to make it impossible to hear the ringtone I'd chosen for it.

I pulled it out of the pocket, putting it on my ear after pressing the green button.

"Yes?" I had to remain calm and composed, even on an occasion where it most likely seemed he was going to verbally abuse me.

If only I didn't have to depend on him to pay the bills and the rent of the shitty flat where I still lived with my sister. As soon as our parents died, we lost our house.

Through some legal loopholes, our asshole uncle managed to snag it for himself. And the worst thing about it was that he wasn't even living there.

I couldn't hide my frustration, anger bubbling up in my blood.

"I've got some good news. You can leave now, if you want. You don't need to stay until after we are closed to help with cleaning it."

I felt my heart jumping, trying to figure out if I'd heard that right.

"Are you sure? This has never happened before."

"Yeah, I am. I just thought that you needed to relax a little, maybe go out tonight with your boyfriend to some bar, and kick back with him."

I never told him that I didn't have a boyfriend. It was no wonder he was assuming, once again, that I had one.

I quickly recomposed myself, straightening my back. I was going to take everything I could to have a slightly better night, even though that still meant turning on the TV and pretending that there was something good being played on it.

"Uhhh, thank you, sir. I appreciate it."

"Then, go have some fun. I'm sure you have some plans, but," he paused, breathing in loudly, "if you find yourself thinking that your boyfriend is a huge waste of time, you know where to find me."

And there he was, hitting on me again. It had happened a lot of times in the past, and it was one of the many reasons to walk out of this establishment one day and never look back.

"I… don't think that will be necessary," I affirmed, ending the call after he wished me to have a good time with whatever I was going to do with my boyfriend.

I actually liked that he didn't know much about me, still thinking that I had a normal life like everyone else.

If there was one thing I was thinking about doing tonight that I usually didn't, it was whipping up something special for dinner.

Now that I had more time, maybe I could do that…

SIMILAR BOOKS

SERIES - ALPHA HUNTERS

1. Not my Wedding
2. Not my Vows
3. Not his Baby
4. Not my Fiancé
5. Not my Daughter

SERIES - RUTHLESS MAFIOSOS

1. His Accidental Triplets
2. His Sweet Captive
3. His Stolen Bride
4. His Accidental Baby
5. His Secret Triplets
6. His Fleeing Single Mom
7. Not my Daughter
8. Not my Fiancé

ABOUT THE AUTHOR

Ruthless mafiosos, gorgeous billionaires, and feisty heroines are just tiny fractions of Jolie Damman's stories. She breathes and lives dark romance, peppering each scene with intrigue and tension that sweep readers away.

When she isn't writing, she's reading by the fireplace of her house as she takes sips of her tea.

9 798838 836588